Daisy Miller

Henry James

HELBLING LANGUAGES

www.helblinglanguages.com

Daisy Miller
by Henry James
© HELBLING LANGUAGES 2007

All rights reserved. No part of this publication may be reproduced, stored in a retrieval system, or transmitted, in any form or by any means, electronic, mechanical, photocopying, recording, or otherwise, without the prior written permission of the Publishers.

First published 2007

ISBN 978-3-85272-010-4

The publishers would like to thank the following for their kind permission to reproduce the following photographs and other copyright material: Alamy p 6.

Series editor Maria Cleary
Adapted by Janet Olearski
Illustrated by Francesca Protopapa
Activities by Janet Olearski
Design by Capolinea
Layout by Pixarte
Printed by Athesia

About this Book

For the Student

🎧 Listen to the story and do some activities on your Audio CD

🎧 End of the listening excerpt

▷ Talk about the story

inn • When you see the orange dot you can check the word in the glossary

For the Teacher

Go to our Readers Resource site for information on using readers and downloadable Resource Sheets, photocopiable Worksheets, Answer Keys and Tapescripts. Plus the full version of the story on MP3.

www.helblinglanguages.com/readers

For lots of great ideas on using Graded Readers consult Reading Matters, the Teacher's Guide to using Helbling Readers.

Level 5 Structures

Modal verb *would*	Non-defining relative clauses
I'd love to …	Present perfect continuous
Future continuous	*Used to / would*
Present perfect future	*Used to / used to doing*
Reported speech / verbs/ questions	Second conditional
Past perfect	Expressing wishes and regrets
Defining relative clauses	

Structures from lower levels are also included.

3

Contents

About the Author	6
Before Reading	8
Daisy Miller	11
After Reading	76

About the Author

Henry James was born in New York in 1843 into a wealthy, intellectual family. He was named after his father, Henry James Senior, who was a well-known theologian. When he was a child James travelled with his family back and forth between Europe and America, studying with tutors for the time he was abroad.

James loved reading and could read fluently in French, Italian and German as well as his native English. In 1864, he anonymously published his first short story, *A Tragedy of Error*, and from then on devoted himself completely to literature. Throughout his career, he wrote extensively, publishing books and articles in a variety of genres: novels, short story collections, literary criticism, travel writing, biography and autobiography. In all, he wrote 22 novels, including two left unfinished at his death, and 112 stories, along with many plays and essays.

James moved to Europe, settling permanently in England in 1876. He lived there, first in London then in Rye, in Sussex. The outbreak of World War I was a profound shock for James, and in 1915, he became a British citizen to declare his loyalty to his adopted country as well as to protest against America's refusal to enter the war on behalf of Britain. James died in London in 1916. He is considered by many writers and critics to be one of the greatest American authors and a number of his works have been made into successful films.

About the Author

Daisy Miller was first published in the June and July 1878 issues of *Cornhill* magazine, in Britain. It was an immediate success and gained James a reputation as an international author. The story is based on a piece of gossip that James recorded in his notebook.

It tells the story of a pretty young American girl, the Daisy Miller of the title, who is travelling around Europe with her mother and younger brother. Daisy meets a compatriot, Winterbourne, who is fascinated by her open and friendly manner. However, Daisy's flirtatiousness is frowned upon by the other expatriates they meet and her lack of understanding of the unsaid rules of society ultimately leads to tragedy.

The novella explores a number of themes which James continued to explore in his later novels. It is one of his earliest treatments of the behaviour of Americans abroad. In the years following the American Civil War a new business class emerged and they soon were eager to further their children's education by taking them on the 'grand tour' of Europe. James was drawn to the innocence and freshness of his compatriots while he also felt they were undereducated and provincial compared to their European counterparts.

It also takes a look at another theme which is central to his work: that of the choice not to live one's life to the full. Throughout James' stories characters realise that what they were waiting for has passed them by and that they have wasted their whole lives, or parts of their lives thinking about it. In *Daisy Miller* Winterbourne spends the entire novel trying to figure out Daisy, without ever understanding her or what she means to him.

Many critics consider *Daisy Miller* to be a preface to James' later novel *Portrait of a Lady*.

Before Reading

1 Before you read the story, take a look at the pictures in the book and on the cover. Write a list of ten words or expressions that you think will describe the story you are going to read. If possible, work with a partner and compare your lists.

2 The title of the story is *Daisy Miller*. What type of story do you think it will be and what do you think it will be about? Discuss the ideas below in groups of three or four.

   a) A love story. A young woman called Daisy will fall in love and get married.
   b) A tragedy. Daisy will make a serious mistake and someone will die as a result.
   c) A mystery. Daisy will be involved in a series of mysterious events.
   d) A family drama. There will be conflict between members of Daisy's family.
   e) A travel story. Daisy will go on a long journey, and learn about life in the process.

Share your ideas with the rest of the class.

3 Look at this picture of Daisy Miller. What do you think she is like? Write down questions you would like to ask her. Ask and answer with a partner.

Before Reading

4 Imagine that you are the parents of a 16-year-old girl. What would you allow her to do and what would you *not* allow her to do? Write a list.
Now imagine that you are the parents of a 16-year-old boy. Make a list of the things that you would allow him to do and the things you *wouldn't* allow him to do.
Are your two lists the same or different?

5 On a scale of 1 to 5 (1 = I don't agree at all; 5 = I agree entirely) how far do you agree with the following statements?

a) Living for a long time in a foreign country helps you become more open-minded.
1 ☐   **2** ☐   **3** ☐   **4** ☐   **5** ☐

b) When you live in a foreign country, you should behave just as you would in your own country.
1 ☐   **2** ☐   **3** ☐   **4** ☐   **5** ☐

c) You should be careful not to offend people by doing things they don't approve of.
1 ☐   **2** ☐   **3** ☐   **4** ☐   **5** ☐

d) If you love a person, their upbringing and social class are not important.
1 ☐   **2** ☐   **3** ☐   **4** ☐   **5** ☐

e) Men can make friends with anyone they like, but women cannot.
1 ☐   **2** ☐   **3** ☐   **4** ☐   **5** ☐

Daisy Miller

I

In the little town of Vevey, in Switzerland, there is a most comfortable hotel, which is seated upon the edge of a clear blue lake. The shore of the lake has a range of establishments* of this type. One of the hotels, however, is famous, being distinguished* from many of its neighbours by an air both of luxury and of maturity. In this region, in the month of June, American travellers are extremely numerous. There is a flitting* here and there of 'stylish' young girls, a rustling* of muslin* frills, a rattle of dance music in the morning hours, a sound of high-pitched* voices at all times. You receive an impression of these things at the excellent inn* of the 'Trois Couronnes'.

I hardly know what was in the mind of a young American, who, two or three years ago, sat in the garden of the 'Trois Couronnes', looking about him, rather idly, at some of the graceful objects I have mentioned. He had come from Geneva the day before by the little steamer*, to see his aunt, who was staying at the hotel – Geneva having been for a long time his place of residence. But his aunt had a headache – his aunt had almost always a headache – and now she was closed in her room, so that he was at liberty to wander about.

Glossary

- **distinguished:** (here) shown to be different
- **establishments:** (here) hotels
- **flitting:** moving about quickly from place to place
- **high-pitched:** with a high and sharp tone
- **inn:** guest house; place where you can sleep and eat
- **muslin:** thin, semi-transparent material used to make dresses
- **rustling:** sound that some materials (silk and muslin) make
- **steamer:** ship with a steam-driven engine

He was some seven-and-twenty years of age. His friends usually said that he was in Geneva 'studying'. Other people said that the reason he spent so much time in Geneva was that he was extremely devoted to a lady who lived there – a foreign lady – a person older than himself. Very few Americans had ever seen this lady, about whom there were some curious stories. Winterbourne had gone to school and college in Geneva, and this had led to his forming a great many youthful friendships there. Many of these he had kept, and they were a source of great satisfaction to him.

After learning that his aunt was not feeling well, he had taken a walk about the town, and then he had come in to have breakfast. Now he was drinking a small cup of coffee at a little table in the garden. At last he finished his coffee and lit a cigarette. Soon a small boy of nine or ten came along the path. The child had a pale face, and was dressed in knickerbockers*, with red stockings, which displayed* his poor little thin legs; he also wore a brilliant red cravat*. He carried a long alpenstock*, the sharp point of which he thrust* into everything that he approached – the flowerbeds, the garden benches, the trains* of the ladies' dresses. In front of Winterbourne he paused, looking at him with a pair of bright, penetrating eyes.

Glossary

- **alpenstock:** a stick carried by mountain walkers
- **cravat:** informal neck-tie
- **displayed:** showed
- **knickerbockers:** old-fashioned short trousers often worn by young boys
- **thrust:** pushed with great force or power
- **trains:** (here) long pieces of material at the back of ladies' dresses

Daisy Miller

'Will you give me a lump* of sugar?' he asked in a hard little voice.

Winterbourne glanced at the small table near him and saw that several pieces of sugar remained. 'Yes, you may take one,' he answered; 'but I don't think sugar is good for little boys.'

This little boy carefully selected three lumps of sugar, two of which he buried in the pocket of his knickerbockers, depositing* the other in his mouth. He tried to crack* it with his teeth.

'Oh, it's har-r-d!' he exclaimed, pronouncing the adjective in a peculiar* manner.

Winterbourne had immediately perceived* that he might have the honour of claiming him as a fellow countryman. 'Take care you don't hurt your teeth,' he said, paternally.

'I haven't got any teeth to hurt. I have only got seven teeth. My mother said she'd slap* me if any more came out. It's the climate that makes them come out.'

Winterbourne was greatly amused. 'If you eat three lumps of sugar, your mother will certainly slap you,' he said.

Trois Couronnes, Rue d'Italie, Vevey

CHILDHOOD

Think back to when you were a child. Did you have any habits that annoyed your parents or guardians? What did they say to you?

- **crack:** break
- **depositing:** putting
- **lump:** small piece
- **peculiar:** strange
- **perceived:** realised
- **slap:** hit someone with your hand; smack

'Here comes my sister!' cried the child.

Winterbourne looked along the path and saw a beautiful young lady advancing. She was dressed in white muslin, with a hundred frills, and knots of pale-coloured ribbon•. She had no hat on, but she balanced in her hand a large parasol and she was very pretty.

The little boy had now converted his alpenstock into a vaulting pole•, with which he was springing• about in the gravel• and kicking up the dust.

'Randolph,' said the young lady, 'what *are* you doing?'

'I'm going up the Alps,' replied Randolph. 'This is the way!' And he gave another little jump, scattering• the pebbles• about Winterbourne's ears.

The young lady looked straight at her brother. 'Well, I guess you had better be quiet,' she simply observed.

Winterbourne got up and stepped slowly towards the young girl, throwing away his cigarette. 'This little boy and I have made acquaintance•,' he said, with great politeness.

In Geneva, a young man was not at liberty• to speak to a young unmarried lady except under certain conditions; but here at Vevey, what conditions could be better than these? – a pretty American girl coming and standing in front of you in a garden. This pretty American girl, however, simply glanced at him; she then turned her head and looked over the parapet•, at the lake and the opposite mountains. Winterbourne wondered whether he had gone too far, but he decided that he must advance farther, rather than retreat. While he was thinking of something else to say, the young lady turned to the little boy again.

Glossary

- **at liberty:** allowed
- **gravel:** many pebbles laid as a smooth surface
- **made acquaintance:** got to know each other
- **parapet:** low wall or balcony
- **pebbles:** small stones
- **ribbon:** a long piece or strip of material used for decoration
- **scattering:** throwing around
- **springing:** (here) jumping
- **vaulting pole:** a stick used to help someone jump over something

'I should like to know where you got that pole,' she said.
'I bought it,' responded Randolph.
'You don't mean you're going to take it to Italy?'
'Yes, *I am* going to take it to Italy,' the child declared.
'Are you going to Italy?' Winterbourne inquired in a tone of great respect.

The young lady glanced at him again. 'Yes, sir,' she replied.
'Are you going over the Simplon?' Winterbourne pursued*, a little embarrassed.

'I don't know,' she said. 'I suppose it's some mountain. Randolph, what mountain are we going over?'

'I don't know,' said Randolph. 'I don't want to go to Italy. I want to go to America.'

'Oh, Italy is a beautiful place!' answered the young man.

Trois Couronnes, Rue d'Italie, Vevey

TRAVEL

Have you ever travelled abroad?
What did you like about the places you visited?
What did you miss about home?

Glossary

- **pursued:** (here) continued

Daisy Miller

The young lady inspected her dress and smoothed * her ribbons. Winterbourne was ceasing to be embarrassed, for he had begun to notice that she was not at all embarrassed herself. There had not been the slightest change in her charming complexion *; she was evidently neither offended nor flattered *. If she looked another way when he spoke to her, and seemed not particularly to hear him, this was simply her manner *. Yet, as he talked a little more and pointed out some of the objects of interest in the view, with which she appeared quite unacquainted *, she gradually gave him more of the benefit of her glance; and then he saw that this glance was perfectly direct. The young girl's eyes were honest and fresh. They were wonderfully pretty eyes. Winterbourne had a great relish * for feminine beauty; he was addicted to observing and analyzing it. He thought it very possible that Master Randolph's sister was a coquette *; he was sure she had a spirit of her own; but in her bright, sweet, superficial little face there was no mockery *, no irony.

Before long it became obvious that she was much disposed towards * conversation. She told him that they were going to Rome for the winter – she and her mother and Randolph. She told him she was from New York State – 'if you know where that is.' Winterbourne caught hold of her small brother and made him stand a few minutes by his side.

'Tell me your name, my boy,' he said. 'Randolph C. Miller,' said the boy sharply. 'And her name is Daisy Miller!' cried the child. 'But that isn't her real name. Her real name is Annie P. Miller.'

- **complexion:** (here) face
- **coquette:** a woman who flirts or behaves in a playful way to make herself attractive to men
- **disposed towards:** liked doing
- **flattered:** (here) felt complimented
- **manner:** way of behaving
- **mockery:** when you make fun of someone in a cruel way
- **relish:** joyful appreciation
- **smoothed:** made flat
- **unacquainted:** not familiar (with)

'Ask him *his* name,' said his sister, indicating Winterbourne.

But on this point Randolph seemed perfectly indifferent; he continued to supply information regarding his own family. 'My father's name is Ezra B. Miller,' he announced. 'My father's in Schenectady. He's got a big business. My father's rich, you bet*!'

'Well!' exclaimed Miss Miller, lowering her parasol and looking at the embroidered* border*. Winterbourne released the child, who departed, dragging* his alpenstock along the path.

'He doesn't like Europe,' said the young girl. 'He wants to go back. Mother's going to get a teacher for him as soon as we get to Italy. Can you get good teachers in Italy?'

'Very good, I should think,' said Winterbourne.

'Or else she's going to find some school. He ought to learn some more. He's only nine. He's going to college.' And in this way Miss Miller continued to converse upon the affairs of her family and upon other topics. She sat there with her extremely pretty hands folded in her lap*, and with her pretty eyes now resting upon those of Winterbourne, now wandering over the garden, the people who passed by, and the beautiful view. She talked to Winterbourne as if she had known him a long time. He found it very pleasant. It was many years since he had heard a young girl talk so much. She was very quiet; she sat in a charming, tranquil attitude, but her lips and her eyes were constantly moving. She had a soft, slender*, agreeable voice, and her tone was decidedly sociable.

> Glossary

- **border:** edge
- **dragging:** pulling
- **embroidered:** decorated with thread
- **lap:** the flat area at the top of your legs when you are sitting down
- **slender:** (here) light
- **you bet:** you can be sure

Daisy Miller

She gave Winterbourne a history of her movements and intentions and those of her mother and brother, in Europe, and enumerated, in particular, the various hotels at which they had stopped. She declared that the hotels were very good, once you got used to their ways, and that Europe was perfectly sweet.

'The only thing I don't like,' she proceeded, 'is the society•. There isn't any society; or, if there is, I don't know where it keeps itself. Do you? I'm very fond of society, and I have always had a great deal of it. I don't mean only in Schenectady, but in New York. I used to go to New York every winter. In New York I had lots of society. I have more friends in New York than in Schenectady – more gentleman friends; and more young lady friends too.' She was looking at Winterbourne with all her prettiness in her lively eyes and in her light, slightly monotonous• smile. 'I have always had plenty of gentlemen's society.'

• **monotonous:** boring

• **society:** (here) the company of different, rich, fashionable people

19

Poor Winterbourne was amused, perplexed •, and decidedly charmed. He had never yet heard a young girl express herself in just this fashion. He felt that he had lived at Geneva so long that he had lost a great deal •; he had become unaccustomed to the American tone. Never, indeed, since he had grown old enough to appreciate things, had he encountered a young American girl of so pronounced a type • as this. Certainly she was very charming, but how sociable! Was she simply a pretty girl from New York State? Were they all like that, the pretty girls who had a good deal of gentlemen's society? Or was she also a designing •, an audacious •, an unscrupulous • young person?

Winterbourne had lost his instinct in this matter, and his reason could not help him. Miss Daisy Miller looked extremely innocent. Some people had told him that American girls were exceedingly innocent; and others had told him that they were not. He was inclined to think Miss Daisy Miller was a flirt – a pretty American flirt. He had never, as yet, had any relations with young ladies of this category. He had known, here in Europe, two or three women – persons older than Miss Daisy Miller, and provided, for respectability's sake, with husbands – who were great coquettes. They were dangerous, terrible women, with whom one's relations were liable to take a serious turn •. But this young girl was not a coquette in that sense; she was very unsophisticated •; she was only a pretty American flirt.

Glossary

- **audacious:** bold
- **courier:** (here) servant who helps with with travel arrangements, etc.
- **designing:** planning, possibly in a dishonest way
- **great deal:** (here) lot
- **of so pronounced a type:** with such a definite personality

- **perplexed:** confused and unsure
- **placidly:** calmly
- **relations were liable to take a serious turn:** friendships would probably become more serious than he wanted
- **unscrupulous:** dishonest; prepared to act in a dishonest way
- **unsophisticated:** simple

Daisy Miller

'Have you been to that old castle?' asked the young girl, pointing with her parasol to the walls of the Chateau de Chillon.

'Yes, more than once,' said Winterbourne. 'You too, I suppose, have seen it?'

'No, we haven't been there. I want to go there very much indeed.'

'It's a very pretty excursion,' said Winterbourne. 'You can drive, you know, or you can go by the little steamer. I should think it might be arranged,' said Winterbourne. 'Couldn't you get someone to stay for the afternoon with Randolph?'

Miss Miller looked at him a moment, and then, very placidly•, 'I wish *you* would stay with him!' she said.

Winterbourne hesitated a moment. 'I should much rather go to Chillon with you.'

'With me?' asked the young girl with the same placidity.

'With your mother,' he answered very respectfully.

'Then we may arrange it. If mother will stay with Randolph, I guess Eugenio will stay too.'

'Eugenio?' the young man inquired.

'Eugenio's our courier•. He doesn't like staying with Randolph, but I guess he'll stay with him if mother does, and then we can go to the castle.'

Winterbourne reflected for an instant – 'we' could only mean Miss Daisy Miller and himself. This programme seemed almost too delightful to believe; he felt as if he ought to kiss the young lady's hand, but at this moment another person, presumably Eugenio, appeared.

A tall, handsome man, with a superb moustache, wearing a velvet morning coat and a brilliant watch chain, approached Miss Miller, looking sharply at her companion.

'Oh, Eugenio!' said Miss Miller with the friendliest accent.

Eugenio had looked at Winterbourne from head to foot; he now bowed* gravely* to the young lady. 'I have the honour to inform mademoiselle that luncheon* is upon the table.'

Miss Miller slowly rose. 'See here, Eugenio!' she said; 'I'm going to that old castle, anyway.'

'To the Chateau de Chillon, mademoiselle?' the courier inquired. 'Mademoiselle has made arrangements?' he added in a tone which struck Winterbourne as very rude. The young girl turned to Winterbourne, blushing* a little.

'You won't back out*?' she said.

'I shall not be happy till we go!' he protested.

'And you are staying in this hotel?' she went on. 'Are you really an American?'

The courier stood looking at Winterbourne offensively*. Winterbourne thought his manner of looking at Miss Miller showed disapproval, as she 'picked up*' acquaintances.

'I shall have the honor of presenting to you a person who will tell you all about me,' he said, smiling and referring to his aunt.

She gave him a smile and turned away. She put up her parasol and walked back to the inn beside Eugenio. Winterbourne stood looking after her; and as she moved away, said to himself that she appeared as elegant as a princess.

Trois Couronnes, Rue d'Italie, Vevey

DAISY MILLER

What does Winterbourne think of Daisy Miller?

Glossary

- **back out:** change (one's) mind; reverse a decision
- **blushing:** turning pink or red with embarrassment
- **bowed:** bent his head and body in respect
- **gravely:** in a serious way
- **luncheon:** (old-fashioned) lunch
- **offensively:** in a way that offends or embarrasses someone
- **picked up:** got to know people without being formally introduced to them

He had, however, promised to do more than proved[•] possible, in promising to present his aunt, Mrs Costello, to Miss Daisy Miller. In his aunt's apartment, after making the proper inquiries in regard to her health, he asked if she had observed in the hotel an American family – a mamma, a daughter, and a little boy.

'And a courier?' said Mrs Costello. 'Oh yes, I have observed them, seen them, heard them, and kept out of their way.' Mrs Costello was a widow with a fortune; a person of much distinction. She had two sons married in New York and another who was now in Europe. This young man was amusing himself in Hamburg, and rarely visited any particular city at the moment selected by his mother for her own appearance there. Her nephew, who had come up to Vevey especially to see her, was therefore more attentive[•] than those who, as she said, were nearer to her. Mrs Costello had not seen him for many years, and she was greatly pleased with him.

He immediately noted, from her tone, that Miss Daisy Miller's place in the social scale was low.

'I am afraid you don't approve of them,' he said.

'They are very common[•],' Mrs Costello declared.

'Ah, you don't accept them?' said the young man.

'I can't, my dear Frederick. I would if I could, but I can't.'

'The young girl is very pretty,' said Winterbourne.

'Of course she's pretty. But she is very common. She has that charming look that they all have,' his aunt resumed, 'and she dresses perfectly. I can't think where they get their taste[•]. They treat the courier like a familiar friend – like a gentleman. I shouldn't wonder if he dines[•] with them. Very likely they have never seen a man with such good manners,

---

Glossary

- **attentive:** giving attention
- **common:** (here) of a low social standing
- **dines:** eats
- **proved:** (here) was
- **taste:** (here) style

Daisy Miller

such fine clothes, so like a gentleman. He probably corresponds to the young lady's idea of a count. He sits with them in the garden in the evening. I think he smokes.'

Winterbourne listened with interest to these disclosures •; they helped him to make up his mind about Miss Daisy. Evidently she was rather wild.

'Well,' he said, 'I am not a courier, and yet she was very charming to me.'

'You had better have said at first,' said Mrs Costello with dignity, 'that you had made her acquaintance.'

'We simply met in the garden, and we talked a bit. I said I should take the liberty • of introducing her to my admirable aunt.'

'I am much obliged to you.'

'It was to guarantee my respectability •,' said Winterbourne.

'And who is to guarantee hers?'

'Ah, you are cruel!' said the young man. 'She's a very nice young girl. She is completely uncultivated •,' Winterbourne went on. 'But she is wonderfully pretty, and, in short, she is very nice. I am going to take her to the Chateau de Chillon.'

'How long had you known her, may I ask, when this interesting project was formed?'

'I have known her half an hour!' said Winterbourne, smiling.

- **disclosures:** pieces of information
- **guarantee my respectability:** show that I am a serious and honest person
- **take the liberty:** do something that risks not being approved of
- **uncultivated:** not having good manners; not well-educated

25

'Dear me!' cried Mrs Costello. 'What a dreadful girl! You have lived too long out of the country. You will be sure to make some great mistake. You are too innocent.'

'My dear aunt, I am not so innocent,' said Winterbourne, smiling and curling• his moustache.

'You are guilty too, then!'

Winterbourne continued to curl his moustache meditatively. 'You won't let the poor girl know you then?' he asked.

'Is it true that she is going to the Chateau de Chillon with you?'

'I think that she fully intends it.'

'Then, my dear Frederick,' said Mrs Costello, 'I must decline• the honour of her acquaintance. I am an old woman, but I am not too old, thank Heaven, to be shocked!'

Glossary

- **curling:** bending or rolling something
- **decline:** refuse politely

Daisy Miller

'But don't they all do these things – the young girls in America?' Winterbourne inquired.

Mrs Costello stared a moment. 'I should like to see my granddaughters do them!' she declared grimly•.

Though he was impatient• to see Daisy, he hardly knew what he should say to her about his aunt's refusal to become acquainted with her. He found her that evening in the garden, wandering about in the warm starlight. It was ten o'clock. Miss Daisy Miller seemed very glad to see him.

'Have you been all alone?' he asked.

'I have been walking round with mother. But mother gets tired walking round,' she answered. 'She doesn't like to go to bed,' said the young girl. 'She doesn't sleep – not three hours. She's dreadfully nervous.'

• **grimly:** seriously; depressingly

• **impatient:** anxious; wanting something to happen and not being calm enough to wait for it

Winterbourne strolled about with the young girl for some time without meeting her mother.

'I have been looking round for that lady you want to introduce me to,' his companion resumed. 'She's your aunt.'

She had heard all about Mrs Costello from the chambermaid*. She was very quiet, she spoke to no one, and she never dined at the table d'hôte*. Every two days she had a headache.

'I think that's a lovely description, headache and all!' said Miss Daisy, chattering* along in her thin, gay* voice. 'I want to know her ever so much. I know I should like her. She would be very exclusive*. I'm dying to be exclusive myself. Well, we *are* exclusive, mother and I. We don't speak to everyone – or they don't speak to us. I suppose it's about the same thing. Anyway, I shall be ever so glad to know your aunt.'

Winterbourne was embarrassed. 'She would be most happy,' he said; 'but I am afraid those headaches will interfere.'

EXCUSES

Trois Couronnes, Rue d'Italie, Vevey

Have you ever made an excuse when you couldn't or didn't want to do something?
Why did you make it?
Discuss with a partner.

Glossary

- **chambermaid:** woman who cleans hotel rooms
- **chattering:** talking quickly
- **exclusive:** (here) talks to only a few carefully chosen people
- **gay:** happy
- **table d'hôte:** hotel restaurant

Daisy Miller

The young girl looked at him through the dusk. 'But I suppose she doesn't have a headache every day,' she said sympathetically.

Winterbourne was silent a moment. 'She tells me she does,' he answered at last, not knowing what to say.

Miss Daisy Miller stopped and stood looking at him. Her prettiness was still visible in the darkness; she was opening and closing her enormous fan. 'She doesn't want to know me!' she said suddenly. 'Why don't you say so? You needn't be afraid.' And she gave a little laugh.

Winterbourne thought there was a tremor in her voice; he was touched* by it. 'My dear young lady,' he protested, 'she knows no one. It's her bad health.'

The young lady, resuming her walk, gave an exclamation in quite another tone. 'Well, here's Mother! I guess she hasn't got Randolph to go to bed.' The figure of a lady appeared at a distance, very indistinct in the darkness, and advancing with a slow movement.

'I am afraid your mother doesn't see you,' said Winterbourne.

'She won't come here because she sees you.'

'Ah, then,' said Winterbourne, 'I had better leave you. I'm afraid your mother doesn't approve of my walking with you.'

Miss Miller gave him a serious glance. 'Mother doesn't like any of my gentlemen friends. She always makes a fuss* if I introduce a gentleman. But I *do* introduce them – almost always.'

By this time they had come up to Mrs Miller, who, as they drew near, walked to the parapet of the garden and leaned upon it, looking intently at the lake and turning her back to them.

---

* **fuss:** excitement or worry, usually unneeded

* **touched:** it made him feel warm and good

'Mother!' said the young girl in a tone of decision.

The elder lady turned round. 'Mr Winterbourne,' said Miss Daisy Miller, introducing the young man very frankly • and prettily. 'Common,' she was, as Mrs Costello had said; yet it was a wonder to Winterbourne that, with her commonness, she had a singularly delicate grace.

Her mother was a small person, with a wandering eye, a very small nose, and a large forehead, decorated with frizzled • hair. Like her daughter, Mrs Miller was dressed with extreme elegance; she had enormous diamonds in her ears. She gave Winterbourne no greeting – she certainly was not looking at him.

'I was telling Mr Winterbourne about Randolph,' the young girl went on.

'Oh, yes!' said Winterbourne; 'I have the pleasure of knowing your son.'

'I think Randolph's real tiresome •,' Daisy pursued.

'Well, Daisy Miller,' said the elder lady, 'I shouldn't think you'd want to talk against your own brother!'

'Well, he wouldn't go to that castle,' said the young girl. 'I'm going there with Mr Winterbourne.'

To this announcement, Daisy's mamma offered no response. Winterbourne took for granted that she deeply disapproved of the projected excursion; but he said to himself that she was a simple, easily managed person, and that a few deferential • protestations • would take the edge from her displeasure.

'Yes,' he began, 'your daughter has kindly allowed me the honour of being her guide.'

'We've been thinking ever so much about going,' she pursued; 'but it seems as if we couldn't. Of course Daisy – she wants to go round. We visited several castles in England,' she added.

Glossary

- **deferential:** polite
- **frankly:** openly
- **frizzled:** curly (not nice)
- **protestations:** strong declarations
- **real tiresome:** very boring; irritating

Daisy Miller

'Ah yes! In England there are beautiful castles,' said Winterbourne. 'But Chillon, here, is very well worth seeing•.

'Well, if Daisy feels up to it• –' said Mrs Miller.

'Oh, I think she'll enjoy it!' Winterbourne declared. 'You are not disposed•, madam,' he inquired, 'to undertake• it yourself?'

'Yes, it would be lovely!' said Daisy. But she made no movement to accompany him.

'I should think you had better find out what time it is,' said her mother.

'It is eleven o'clock, madam,' said a voice, with a foreign accent, out of the neighbouring darkness.

'Oh, Eugenio,' said Daisy, 'I am going out in a boat!'

Eugenio bowed. 'At eleven o'clock, mademoiselle?'

'I am going with Mr Winterbourne – this very minute•.'

'Do tell her she can't,' said Mrs Miller to the courier.

'I think you had better not go out in a boat, mademoiselle,' Eugenio declared.

'I suppose you don't think it's proper•!' Daisy exclaimed. 'Eugenio doesn't think anything's proper.'

'Does mademoiselle propose to go alone?' asked Eugenio of Mrs Miller.

'Oh, no; with this gentleman!' answered Daisy's mamma.

The courier looked for a moment at Winterbourne and then, solemnly•, with a bow, 'As mademoiselle pleases!' he said.

'Oh, I hoped you would make a fuss!' said Daisy. 'I don't care to go now. That's all I want – a little fuss!' And the young girl began to laugh again. 'Mr Randolph has gone to bed!' the courier announced coldly.

'Oh, Daisy, now we can go!' said Mrs Miller.

- **disposed:** interested in
- **feel up to it:** feels she is physically able to do it
- **proper:** correct (behaviour)
- **solemnly:** seriously
- **this very minute:** right now
- **undertake:** (here) go on the trip
- **well worth seeing:** enjoyable and interesting to see

Daisy turned away from Winterbourne, looking at him, smiling and fanning* herself. 'Good night,' she said; 'I hope you are disappointed, or disgusted, or something!'

He looked at her, taking the hand she offered him. 'I am puzzled*,' he answered.

'Well, I hope it won't keep you awake!' she said very smartly*; and, under the escort of the lucky Eugenio, the two ladies passed towards the house.

Winterbourne stood looking after them; he was indeed puzzled.

Two days afterward he went with her to the Castle of Chillon. He waited for her in the large hall of the hotel, where the couriers, the servants, the foreign tourists, were lounging about* and staring. It was not the place he should have chosen, but she had decided upon it. She came tripping* downstairs, buttoning her long gloves, squeezing her folded parasol against her pretty figure*, dressed in an elegant travelling costume. Winterbourne was a man of imagination and as he looked at

Glossary

- **elope:** run away to get married secretly
- **fanning:** moving a fan to cool down
- **figure:** body
- **lounging about:** sitting lazily
- **puzzled:** confused; not able to understand (something)
- **smartly:** quickly
- **tripping:** (here) walking with a light step

Daisy Miller

her dress and, on the great staircase, her little rapid step, he felt as if there were something romantic happening. He could have believed he was going to elope* with her. He passed out with her among all the idle people that were assembled there; they were all looking at her very hard; she had begun to chatter as soon as she joined him.

She expressed a lively wish to go to Chillon in the little steamer; she declared that she had a passion for steamboats. There was always such a lovely breeze upon the water, and you saw such a lot of people. The voyage was not long, but Winterbourne's companion found time to say a great many things. People continued to look at her a great deal, and Winterbourne took much satisfaction in his pretty companion's distinguished air. He had been a little afraid that she would talk loudly, laugh too much. But he quite forgot his fears; he sat smiling, with his eyes upon her face, while, she made a great number of original remarks. He had agreed to the idea that she was 'common'; but was she, or was he simply getting used to her commonness?

In the castle, Daisy tripped about the vaulted chambers*, rustled her skirts in the corkscrew* staircases, flirted back with a pretty little cry and a shudder* from the edge of the oubliettes*, and turned a well-shaped ear to everything that Winterbourne told her about the place. They had the good fortune to walk about without other company than that of the custodian*; and Winterbourne arranged with him that they should not be hurried. The custodian* interpreted the arrangement generously – Winterbourne, on his side, had been generous – and left them quite* to themselves. Miss Miller found a great many reasons for asking Winterbourne sudden questions about himself – his family, his previous history, his tastes, his habits, his intentions. Of her own tastes, habits, and intentions Miss Miller was prepared to give the most definite, and indeed the most favourable account.

Daisy went on to say that she wished Winterbourne would travel with them. Winterbourne said that nothing could possibly please him so much, but that he unfortunately had other occupations.

'What do you mean?' said Miss Daisy, 'You are not in business.' The young man admitted that he was not in business; but he had engagements* which would force him to go back to Geneva.

'Well, Mr Winterbourne,' said Daisy, 'I think you're horrid*!'

'Oh, don't say such dreadful* things!' said Winterbourne.

'I have half a mind to leave you here and go straight back to the hotel alone.' And for the next ten minutes she did nothing but call him horrid.

Glossary

- **corkscrew:** winding shape or having a spiral shape like the metal piece used to take corks out of bottles
- **custodian:** guardian
- **dreadful:** terrible; awful
- **engagements:** appointments; meetings
- **horrid:** horrible
- **oubliettes:** deep dungeons in which prisoners were left and forgotten about
- **quite:** (here) completely
- **shudder:** tremble with fear
- **vaulted chambers:** rooms with arched (rounded) ceilings

Daisy Miller

Poor Winterbourne was bewildered•; no young lady had ever been so agitated by his movements. His companion, after this, opened fire• upon the mysterious lady in Geneva whom she claimed that he was hurrying back to see. How did Miss Daisy Miller know that there was a charmer in Geneva? Winterbourne, who denied the existence of such a person, was quite unable to discover. She seemed to him an extraordinary mixture of innocence and crudity•.

'Does she never allow you more than three days at a time?' asked Daisy ironically•. 'I suppose, if you stay another day, she'll come after you in the boat.' At last, she told him she would stop 'teasing•' him if he would promise her solemnly to come down to Rome in the winter.

'That's not a difficult promise to make,' said Winterbourne. 'My aunt has taken an apartment in Rome for the winter and has already asked me to come and see her.'

'I don't want you to come for your aunt,' said Daisy; 'I want you to come for me.'

He declared that he would certainly come. After this Daisy stopped teasing. Winterbourne took a carriage, and they drove back to Vevey in the dusk•.

In the evening Winterbourne mentioned to Mrs Costello that he had spent the afternoon at Chillon with Miss Daisy Miller.

'She went with you all alone?'

'All alone.'

Mrs Costello sniffed• a little at her smelling bottle•. 'And that,' she exclaimed, 'is the young person whom you wanted me to know!'

- **bewildered:** confused
- **crudity:** rudeness
- **dusk:** evening; when the light has almost gone
- **ironically:** sarcastically
- **opened fire:** attacked

- **smelling bottle:** a bottle containing chemicals with a very strong smell that can revive people who feel ill
- **sniffed:** smelled; took in air through (her) nose
- **teasing:** making fun of (someone) so that they feel embarrassed

II

Winterbourne, who had returned to Geneva the day after his excursion to Chillon, went to Rome towards the end of January. His aunt had been there for several weeks, and he had received a couple of letters from her.

'Those people you were so devoted to last summer at Vevey have turned up here, courier and all,' she wrote. 'They seem to have made several acquaintances. The young lady, however, is very intimate with some third-rate* Italians, with whom she associates in a way that makes much talk.'

Winterbourne, on arriving in Rome, would have discovered Mrs Miller's address and he would have gone to pay his compliments to Miss Daisy.

'After what happened at Vevey, I may certainly call upon* them,' he said to Mrs Costello.

'If, after what happens – at Vevey and everywhere – you desire to keep up the acquaintance, you are very welcome. Of course a man may know everyone. Men are welcome to the privilege*!'

MEN AND WOMEN — Trois Couronnes, Rue d'Italie, Vevey

Do you think society expects women to behave in a different way to men?

Glossary

- **call upon:** visit
- **privilege:** benefit; something good you are allowed
- **third-rate:** unpleasant and common

Daisy Miller

'Pray what happens – here, for instance?' Winterbourne demanded.

'The girl goes about alone with her foreigners. As to what happens further, you must apply elsewhere for information. She has picked up half a dozen* of the regular Roman fortune hunters*, and she takes them about to people's houses. When she comes to a party she brings with her a gentleman with a good deal of manner* and a wonderful moustache.'

'And where is the mother?'

'I haven't the least idea. They are very dreadful people.'

Winterbourne meditated a moment. 'They are very ignorant – very innocent – but they are not bad.'

'They are hopelessly vulgar*,' said Mrs Costello. 'Whether or not being hopelessly vulgar is being 'bad' is a question for philosophers. They are bad enough to dislike, at any rate; and for this short life that is quite enough.'

The news that Daisy Miller was surrounded by half a dozen wonderful moustaches checked* Winterbourne's impulse to go at once to see her. He was annoyed at hearing of a state of affairs* so little in harmony with an image that had lately flitted* in and out of his own meditations; the image of a very pretty girl looking out of an old Roman window and asking herself urgently when Mr Winterbourne would arrive. He determined to wait a little before reminding Miss Miller of his claims to her attention, and he went to call upon other friends.

- **checked:** stopped
- **flitted:** moved lightly and quickly
- **fortune hunters:** men who hope to marry young women who have lots of money
- **half a dozen:** six
- **manner:** (here) way of behaving that makes people notice him
- **state of affairs:** situation; event
- **vulgar:** with unacceptably showy manners and taste (opposite of elegant)

One of these was Mrs Walker, an American lady who had spent several winters in Geneva, where she had placed her children at school. She was a very accomplished * woman, and she lived in the Via Gregoriana. Winterbourne found her in a little red drawing room, filled with southern sunshine. He had not been there ten minutes when the servant came in, announcing 'Madame Mila!' This announcement was soon followed by the entrance of little Randolph Miller, who stopped in the middle of the room and stood staring at Winterbourne. An instant later his pretty sister entered; and then, after a considerable * interval, Mrs Miller slowly advanced.

'I know you!' said Randolph.

'I'm sure you know a great many things,' exclaimed Winterbourne, taking him by the hand. 'How is your education coming on?'

Daisy was exchanging greetings very prettily with her hostess, but when she heard Winterbourne's voice she quickly turned her head. 'Well, I declare *!' she said.

'I told you I should come, you know,' Winterbourne rejoined, smiling.

'You might have * come to see me!' said Daisy.

'I arrived only yesterday.'

'I don't believe that!' the young girl declared.

Winterbourne turned with a protesting smile to her mother, but this lady evaded his glance. Daisy had entered upon a lively conversation with her hostess; Winterbourne judged it becoming * to address a few words to her mother.

'I hope you have been well since we parted at Vevey,' he said.

Mrs Miller now certainly looked at him. 'Not very well, sir,' she answered.

Glossary

- **accomplished:** talented and cultured
- **becoming:** appropriate; the correct thing to do
- **considerable:** fairly long
- **I declare:** I am pleasantly surprised
- **you might have:** (here) you should have

'She's got dyspepsia •,' said Randolph. 'I've got it too. Father's got it. I've got it most!'

This announcement, instead of embarrassing Mrs Miller, seemed to relieve her. 'I suffer from the liver,' she said. 'I think it's this climate.'

Winterbourne had a good deal of gossip • with Mrs Miller, during which Daisy chattered continually to her hostess. The young man asked Mrs Miller how she liked Rome.

'Well, I must say I am disappointed,' she answered. 'We had heard so much about it; I suppose we had heard too much. We had been led to expect something different.'

'Ah, wait a little, and you will become very fond of it,' said Winterbourne.

'I hate it worse and worse every day!' cried Randolph.

'But we have seen places,' resumed his mother, 'that I should put a long way before Rome.' And in reply to Winterbourne's interrogation, 'Zurich is lovely; and we hadn't heard half so much about it.'

Winterbourne expressed the hope that her daughter at least found some gratification • in Rome, and she declared that Daisy was quite carried away •.

'It's on account of • the society – the society's splendid. She has made a great number of acquaintances. I must say they have been very sociable; they have taken her right in •. And then she knows a great many gentlemen. Oh, she thinks there's nothing like Rome. Of course, it's a great deal pleasanter for a young lady if she knows plenty of gentlemen.'

Glossary

- **carried away:** very excited (by something)
- **dyspepsia:** indigestion
- **gossip:** light conversation
- **gratification:** enjoyment
- **on account of:** because of
- **taken her right in:** completely accepted her

Daisy Miller

By this time Daisy had turned her attention again to Winterbourne. 'I've been telling Mrs Walker how mean* you were!' the young girl announced.

'And what is the evidence you have offered?' asked Winterbourne.

'Why, you were awfully* mean at Vevey,' said Daisy. 'You wouldn't stay there when I asked you.'

'My dearest young lady,' cried Winterbourne, with eloquence*, 'have I come all the way to Rome to be criticised by you?'

'Well, I don't know,' said Daisy, touching Mrs Walker's ribbons. 'Mrs Walker, I want to tell you something. 'You know I'm coming to your party.'

'I am delighted to hear it.'

'I've got a lovely dress!'

'I am very sure of that.'

'But I want to ask a favour – permission to bring a friend.'

'I shall be happy to see any of your friends,' said Mrs Walker, turning with a smile to Mrs Miller.

'Oh, they are not my friends,' answered Daisy's mamma.

'It's an intimate friend of mine – Mr Giovanelli,' said Daisy without a tremor in her clear little voice.

Mrs Walker was silent a moment; she gave a rapid glance at Winterbourne. 'I shall be glad to see Mr Giovanelli,' she then said.

'He's an Italian. He's a great friend of mine; he's the handsomest man in the world – except Mr Winterbourne! He knows plenty of Italians, but he wants to know some Americans. He's tremendously clever. He's perfectly lovely!'

- **awfully:** very
- **mean:** (here) unpleasant; cruel
- **with eloquence:** in a beautiful and expressive way

It was settled that this brilliant personage* should be brought to Mrs Walker's party, and then Mrs Miller prepared to take her leave. 'I guess we'll go back to the hotel,' she said.

'You may go back to the hotel, Mother, but I'm going to take a walk,' said Daisy.

'She's going to walk with Mr Giovanelli,' Randolph proclaimed.

'Alone, my dear - at this hour?' Mrs Walker asked. 'I don't think it's safe, my dear.'

Daisy bent over and kissed her hostess. 'Mrs Walker, you are too perfect,' she said. 'I'm not going alone; I am going to meet a friend.'

'Is it Mr Giovanelli?' asked the hostess.

Winterbourne was watching the young girl; at this question his attention quickened. She stood there, smiling and smoothing her bonnet ribbons; she glanced at Winterbourne, and answered, without a shade of hesitation, 'Mr Giovanelli - the beautiful Giovanelli.'

'My dear young friend,' said Mrs Walker, taking her hand pleadingly*, 'don't walk off to the Pincio* at this hour to meet a beautiful Italian.'

'Gracious me!' Daisy exclaimed, 'I don't intend to do anything improper. There's an easy way to settle* it.' She continued to glance at Winterbourne. 'The Pincio is only a hundred yards distant; and if Mr Winterbourne were as polite as he pretends, he would offer to walk with me!'

Winterbourne's politeness hastened* to affirm* itself. They passed downstairs and at the door Winterbourne saw Mrs Miller's carriage waiting, with the courier seated within.

Glossary

- **affirm:** (here) express
- **hastened:** hurried
- **personage:** important person
- **Pincio:** park where Romans liked to walk
- **pleadingly:** in a way that shows you want something very much
- **settle:** (here) come to an agreement

Daisy Miller

'Goodbye, Eugenio!' cried Daisy; 'I'm going to take a walk.'

As the day was splendid and the traffic of vehicles, walkers, and loungers° numerous, the young Americans found their progress much delayed. This fact was highly agreeable to Winterbourne. The slow moving, idly gazing° Roman crowd bestowed° much attention upon the extremely pretty young foreign lady who was passing through it upon his arm. His own mission was to consign° her to the hands of Mr Giovanelli; but Winterbourne resolved° that he would do no such thing.

- **bestowed:** gave
- **consign:** deliver; give
- **gazing:** looking
- **loungers:** idle people
- **resolved:** decided

'Why haven't you been to see me?' asked Daisy. 'You can't get out of that.'

'I have had the honour of telling you that I have only just stepped out of the train.'

'You must have stayed in the train a good while after it stopped!' cried the young girl with her little laugh.

She began to prattle• about her own affairs. 'We've got splendid rooms at the hotel. We are going to stay all winter, if we don't die of the fever. It's a great deal nicer than I thought. The society's extremely select. There are all kinds – English, and Germans, and Italians. I think I like the English best. But there are some lovely Americans.

Glossary

- **artfully poised:** placed with great care
- **mean:** (here) intend
- **nosegay:** small bunch of flowers
- **nursing his cane:** carefully holding his walking stick
- **prattle:** talk quickly in a silly way
- **run over:** hit by a carriage

Daisy Miller

I never saw anything so hospitable.'

When they had passed the gate of the Pincian Gardens, Miss Miller began to wonder where Mr Giovanelli might be.

'I certainly shall not help you find him,' Winterbourne declared.

'Then I shall find him without you,' cried Miss Daisy.

'You certainly won't leave me!' cried Winterbourne.

She burst into her little laugh. 'Are you afraid you'll get lost – or run over*? But there's Giovanelli, leaning against that tree.'

Winterbourne saw, at some distance, a little man standing with folded arms nursing his cane*. He had a handsome face, an artfully poised* hat, a monocle in one eye, and a nosegay* in his buttonhole. Winterbourne looked at him a moment and then said, 'Do you mean* to speak to that man?'

'Do I mean to speak to him? Why, you don't suppose I mean to communicate by signs?'

'Please understand, then,' said Winterbourne, 'that I intend to remain with you.'

Daisy stopped and looked at him gravely, but with eyes that were prettier than ever. 'I have never allowed a gentleman to dictate to me, or to interfere with anything I do.'

'I think you have made a mistake,' said Winterbourne. 'You should sometimes listen to a gentleman – the right one.'

Daisy began to laugh again. 'I do nothing but listen to gentlemen!' she exclaimed. 'Tell me if Mr Giovanelli is the right one!'

Winterbourne thought him not a bad-looking fellow. But he nevertheless said to Daisy, 'No, he's not the right one.'

Daisy evidently had a natural talent for performing introductions; she mentioned the name of each of her companions to the other. She walked along with one of them on each side of her. Mr Giovanelli, who spoke English very cleverly – Winterbourne afterward learned that he had practised the language upon a great many American heiresses • – spoke a great deal of polite nonsense to her. Giovanelli, of course, had not bargained for • a party of three. But he kept his temper in a manner which suggested far-stretching intentions •.

'He is not a gentleman,' said the young American; 'he is only a clever imitation of one.'

'Nevertheless,' Winterbourne said to himself, 'a nice girl ought to know!' And then he came back to the question of whether Daisy was, in fact, a nice girl. Would a nice girl make a rendezvous • with a presumably low-lived • foreigner? But Daisy continued to present herself as an inscrutable • combination of audacity and innocence.

Glossary

- **bargained for:** (here) expected
- **far-stretching intentions:** long-term plans
- **heiresses:** women who will inherit large amounts of money
- **inscrutable:** in a way that makes it difficult to know what you are thinking or planning
- **low-lived:** of a low social position; disreputable
- **rendezvous:** meeting

Daisy Miller

> **Trois Couronnes, Rue d'Italie, Vevey**
>
> # THINK
>
> Why does Winterbourne think that Giovanelli is 'only a clever imitation of a gentleman'?
>
> What does he think of Daisy and her behaviour?
>
> Do you agree with him?

She had been walking some quarter of an hour, attended by her two cavaliers •, when a carriage that had detached itself from the rest drew up • beside the path. Winterbourne perceived that his friend Mrs Walker was seated inside and was beckoning • to him. Mrs Walker was flushed •; she had an excited air.

'It is really too dreadful,' she said. 'That girl must not do this sort of thing. She must not walk here with you two men. Fifty people have noticed her.'

Winterbourne raised his eyebrows. 'I think it's a pity to make too much fuss about it.'

'It's a pity to let the girl ruin herself!'

'She is very innocent,' said Winterbourne.

'She's very crazy!' said Mrs Walker. 'Did you ever see anything so imbecile • as her mother? I could not sit still for thinking of it. I ordered the carriage and put on my bonnet •, and came here as quickly as possible. Thank Heavens I have found you!'

- **beckoning:** signalling; giving (him) a sign to come
- **bonnet:** soft hat for women
- **cavaliers:** gentlemen accompanying a lady and keeping her safe; knights
- **drew up:** slowed down and stopped
- **flushed:** (here) red in the face
- **imbecile:** stupid

'What do you propose* to do with us?' asked Winterbourne, smiling.

'To ask her to get in, to drive her about here for half an hour, so that the world may see she is not running absolutely wild*, and then to take her safely home.'

'I don't think it's a very happy thought,' said Winterbourne; 'but you can try.'

Mrs Walker tried. Daisy, on learning that Mrs Walker wished to speak to her, retraced her steps with perfect good grace and with Mr Giovanelli at her side. She declared that she was delighted to have a chance to present this gentleman to Mrs Walker. She immediately achieved the introduction, and declared that she had never in her life seen anything so lovely as Mrs Walker's carriage rug.

'I am glad you admire it,' said this lady, smiling sweetly. 'Will you get in and let me put it over you?' said Mrs Walker.

'That would be charming, but it's so enchanting* just as I am!' said Daisy.

'It may be enchanting, dear child, but it is not the custom here,' urged* Mrs Walker.

'Well, it ought to be, then!' said Daisy. 'If I didn't walk I should expire*.'

'You should walk with your mother, dear,' cried the lady, losing patience.

'My mother never walked ten steps in her life. And then,' she added with a laugh, 'I am more than five years old.'

'You are old enough to be more reasonable. You are old enough, dear Miss Miller, to be talked about.'

Glossary

- **enchanting:** charming
- **expire:** (here) die
- **propose:** suggest
- **running wild:** acting in an unsuitable way
- **urged:** said in a convincing way

Daisy Miller

Daisy looked at Mrs Walker, smiling intensely. 'Talked about? What do you mean?'

'Come into my carriage, and I will tell you.'

'I don't think I want to know what you mean,' said Daisy presently.

'Should you prefer being thought a very reckless*　girl?' she demanded.

'Gracious!' exclaimed Daisy. She looked at Mr Giovanelli, then she turned to Winterbourne. There was a little pink flush in her cheek. She was tremendously pretty. 'Does Mr Winterbourne think,' she asked slowly, 'that, to save my reputation, I ought to get into the carriage?'

Winterbourne coloured; for an instant he hesitated. The truth, for Winterbourne, was that Daisy Miller should take Mrs Walker's advice. He looked at her exquisite*　prettiness, and then he said, very gently, 'I think you should get into the carriage.'

Daisy gave a violent laugh. 'If this is improper, Mrs Walker,' she pursued, 'then I am all improper, and you must give me up*. Goodbye. I hope you'll have a lovely ride!' and she turned away.

Mrs Walker sat looking after her, and there were tears in her eyes. 'Get in here, sir,' she said to Winterbourne. The young man answered that he felt bound*　to accompany Miss Miller, whereupon*　Mrs Walker declared that if he refused her this favour she would never speak to him again. Winterbourne overtook Daisy and her companion, and told her that Mrs Walker had made a claim upon his society. Daisy shook his hand, hardly looking at him, while Mr Giovanelli bade him farewell*.

- **bade him farewell:** said goodbye to him
- **bound:** that he had to
- **exquisite:** absolute
- **give me up:** not bother to think about me any more
- **reckless:** extremely careless; (someone who is) not aware that they are doing something that can harm themselves or others
- **whereupon:** and so

49

Daisy Miller

Winterbourne was not in the best possible humour as he took his seat in Mrs Walker's carriage. 'That was not clever of you,' he said candidly *.

'In such a case,' his companion answered, 'I don't wish to be clever; I wish to be earnest *!'

'Well, your earnestness has only offended her. I suspect she meant no harm,' Winterbourne said.

'So I thought a month ago. But she has been going too far *.'

'What has she been doing?'

'Everything that is not done * here. Flirting with any man she could pick up; sitting in corners with mysterious Italians; dancing all the evening with the same partners; receiving visits at eleven o'clock at night. Her mother goes away when visitors come. I'm told that at their hotel everyone is talking about her.'

'The poor girl's only fault is that she is very uncultivated,' said Winterbourne angrily. And he added a request that she should inform him why she had made him enter her carriage.

'I wished to beg you to cease * your relations with Miss Miller – not to flirt with her – to give her no further opportunity to expose herself – to let her alone, in short.'

'I'm afraid I can't do that,' said Winterbourne. 'I like her extremely.'

'All the more reason that you shouldn't help her to make a scandal *.'

'There shall be nothing scandalous in my attentions to her.'

'I have said what I had on my conscience *,' Mrs Walker pursued. 'If you wish to rejoin * the young lady I will put you down.'

Glossary

- **candidly:** honestly
- **cease:** stop
- **earnest:** truthful
- **going too far:** (here) doing things that are too bad
- **had on my conscience:** was thinking about, morally

- **not done:** (here) not supposed to be done
- **rejoin:** (here) go back to
- **scandal:** an event or series of events that shocks people

The carriage was traversing that part of the Pincian Garden that overhangs * the wall of Rome and overlooks the beautiful Villa Borghese. It is bordered by a large parapet, near which there are several seats. One of the seats was occupied by a gentleman and a lady, towards whom Mrs Walker gave a toss of her head *. Winterbourne asked the coachman to stop and Winterbourne descended from the carriage. Then, while he raised his hat, Mrs Walker drove majestically * away. Winterbourne turned his eyes towards Daisy and her cavalier. They evidently saw no one; they were too deeply occupied with each other. Daisy's companion took her parasol out of her hands and opened it. She came a little nearer, and he held the parasol over her so that both of their heads were hidden from Winterbourne. This young man walked towards the residence of his aunt, Mrs Costello.

On the following day, he asked for Mrs Miller at her hotel. This lady and her daughter, however, were not at home. Mrs Walker's party took place on the evening of the third day, and, in spite of the frigidity * of his last interview with the hostess, Winterbourne was among the guests. When he arrived, Daisy Miller was not there, but in a few moments he saw her mother come in alone, very shyly *.

'You see, I've come all alone,' said poor Mrs Miller. 'I'm so frightened. It's the first time I've ever been to a party alone. Daisy just pushed me off * by myself.

Glossary

- **a toss of her head:** a quick movement of the head to indicate where someone or something is
- **frigidity:** coldness
- **majestically:** like a king or queen
- **overhangs:** looks over
- **pushed me off:** sent me away roughly
- **shyly:** timidly

Daisy Miller

'And does not your daughter intend to favour us with her society?' demanded Mrs Walker impressively.

MRS WALKER

Trois Couronnes, Rue d'Italie, Vevey

What is Mrs Walker's attitude to Daisy?

'Well, Daisy's all dressed,' said Mrs Miller. 'But she's got a friend of hers there; that gentleman – the Italian – that she wanted to bring. They've got going• at the piano. Mr Giovanelli sings splendidly. But I guess they'll come soon,' concluded Mrs Miller hopefully.

Daisy came after eleven o'clock. She rustled forward in radiant loveliness, smiling and chattering, carrying a large bouquet•, and attended by Mr Giovanelli. Everyone stopped talking and turned and looked at her. She came straight to Mrs Walker. 'I'm afraid you thought I never was coming, so I sent mother off to tell you. I wanted to make Mr Giovanelli practise some things before he came; you know he sings beautifully, and I want you to ask him to sing. This is Mr Giovanelli; you know I introduced him to you; he's got the most lovely voice, and he knows the most charming set of songs. I made him go over• them this evening on purpose. We had the greatest time at the hotel.' Of all this Daisy delivered• herself, looking now at her hostess and now round the room. 'Is there anyone I know?' she asked.

- **bouquet:** bunch of flowers
- **delivered:** said
- **go over:** practise
- **got going:** (here) started playing

'I think every one knows you!' said Mrs Walker, and she gave a very cursory ° greeting to Mr Giovanelli. This gentleman bore himself gallantly °. He smiled and bowed and showed his white teeth; he curled his moustaches and rolled his eyes and performed all the proper functions of a handsome Italian at an evening party. He sang very prettily half a dozen songs, though Mrs Walker declared that she had been unable to find out who asked him. Daisy sat at a distance from the piano, and though she had publicly professed ° a high admiration for his singing, talked, not inaudibly, while it was going on.

'It's a pity ° these rooms are so small; we can't dance,' she said to Winterbourne.

'I am not sorry we can't dance,' Winterbourne answered; 'I don't dance.'

'Of course you don't dance; you're too stiff °,' said Miss Daisy. 'I hope you enjoyed your drive with Mrs Walker!'

'No. I didn't enjoy it; I preferred walking with you.'

'We paired off °: that was much better,' said Daisy. 'But did you ever hear anything so cool ° as Mrs Walker's wanting me to get into her carriage and drop poor Mr Giovanelli, and under the pretext that it was proper? It would have been most unkind; he had been talking about that walk for ten days.'

'He should not have talked about it at all,' said Winterbourne; 'he would never have proposed to a young lady of this country to walk about the streets with him.'

Glossary

- **bore himself gallantly:** behaved in a well-mannered way
- **cool:** (here) unfriendly
- **cursory:** brief and dismissive
- **fearful, frightful:** terrible
- **it's a pity:** it's not a good thing that
- **paired off:** formed pairs
- **professed:** declared
- **stiff:** rigid; not relaxed

Daisy Miller

'About the streets?' cried Daisy with her pretty stare. 'Where, then, would he have proposed to her to walk? Thank goodness, I am not a young lady of this country. The young ladies of this country have a dreadful time of it, so far as I can learn; I don't see why I should change my habits for *them*.'

'I am afraid your habits are those of a flirt,' said Winterbourne gravely.

'Of course they are,' she cried, 'I'm a fearful, frightful• flirt! Did you ever hear of a nice girl that was not? But I suppose you will tell me now that I am not a nice girl.'

'You're a very nice girl; but I wish you would flirt with me, and me only,' said Winterbourne.

'Ah! Thank you – thank you very much; you are the last man I should think of flirting with.'

'If you won't flirt with me, do cease, at least, to flirt with your friend at the piano; they don't understand that sort of thing here.'

'I thought they understood nothing else!' exclaimed Daisy.

'Not in young unmarried women.'

'It seems to me much more proper in young unmarried women than in old married ones,' Daisy declared.

'Well,' said Winterbourne, 'when you deal with* the inhabitants of a country you must go by the custom of the place. Flirting is a purely American custom; it doesn't exist here. Though you may be flirting, Mr Giovanelli is not; he means something else.'

'If you want very much to know, we are neither of us flirting; we are too good friends for that.'

Trois Couronnes, Rue d'Italie, Vevey

FLIRTING

Winterbourne accuses Daisy of flirting.
What is a flirt? What way do they behave?
Do you think flirting is acceptable or unacceptable?

Glossary

- **deal with:** (here) talk with; interact socially

Daisy Miller

Ah!' answered Winterbourne, 'if you are in love with each other, it is another affair.'

Daisy immediately got up, blushing visibly. 'Mr Giovanelli, at least,' she said, 'never says such very disagreeable things to me.'

Mr Giovanelli had finished singing. He left the piano and came over to Daisy. 'Won't you come into the other room and have some tea?' he asked.

Daisy turned to Winterbourne, beginning to smile again. 'It has never occurred to Mr Winterbourne to offer me any tea,' she said with her little tormenting manner.

'I have offered you advice,' Winterbourne said.

'I prefer weak tea!' cried Daisy, and she went off with the brilliant Giovanelli.

When Daisy came to say goodbye, Mrs Walker turned her back on her and left her to depart with what grace she might. Winterbourne saw it all. Daisy turned very pale and looked at her mother, but Mrs Miller was unconscious of any violation of the usual social forms*. 'Good night, Mrs Walker,' she said; 'we've had a beautiful evening.' Daisy turned away, with a pale, sad face. Winterbourne saw that she was too shocked and puzzled even for indignation*. He on his side was greatly touched.

'That was very cruel,' he said to Mrs Walker.

'She never enters my drawing room* again!' replied his hostess.

- **drawing room:** room where guests are received
- **forms:** (here) rules; expected behaviour
- **indignation:** angry behaviour because of something that has happened

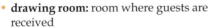

Since Winterbourne was not going to meet Daisy in Mrs Walker's drawing room, he went as often as possible to Mrs Miller's hotel. The ladies were rarely at home, but when he found them, Giovanelli was always present. Very often he was in the drawing room with Daisy alone. Daisy showed no displeasure at her meeting with Giovanelli being interrupted; she could chatter as freely with two gentlemen as with one. She seemed to Winterbourne a girl who would never be jealous. With regard to the women who had hitherto* interested him, it very often seemed to Winterbourne that he should be afraid of these ladies; he had a pleasant sense that he should never be afraid of Daisy Miller. But she was evidently very much interested in Giovanelli. She looked at him whenever he spoke.

One Sunday afternoon, having gone to St. Peter's with his aunt, Winterbourne saw Daisy strolling* about the great church in company with Giovanelli. He pointed out the young girl and her cavalier to Mrs Costello. This lady looked at them a moment through her eyeglass*, and then she said:

'That's what makes you so pensive these days, eh?'

Mrs Costello inspected the young couple again. 'He is very handsome. One easily sees how it is. She thinks him the most elegant man in the world, the finest gentleman. She has never seen anything like him; he is better, even, than the courier. It was the courier probably who introduced him; and if he succeeds in marrying the young lady, the courier will come in for a magnificent commission*.'

'I don't believe she thinks of marrying him,' said Winterbourne, 'and I don't believe he hopes to marry her.'

- **commission:** payment
- **eyeglass:** monocle; a glass for seeing things better
- **hitherto:** up to now; before this time
- **strolling:** walking slowly

58

Daisy Miller

'You can be sure,' said Mrs Costello, 'that she may tell you any moment that she is 'engaged*'.'

'I think that is more than Giovanelli expects,' said Winterbourne.

'Who is Giovanelli?'

'The little Italian. I have asked questions about him. He is apparently a perfectly respectable little man. He is evidently immensely charmed with Miss Miller. She must seem to him wonderfully pretty and interesting. I rather doubt that he dreams of marrying her. He has nothing but his handsome face to offer, and there is a wealthy Mr Miller in that mysterious land of dollars. Giovanelli knows that he hasn't a title to offer. If he were only a count or a *marchese**! He must wonder at his luck, at the way they have taken him up*.'

That day a dozen of the American colonists* in Rome came to talk with Mrs Costello, who sat on a little portable stool at the base of one of the great pilasters* of Saint Peter's. Between Mrs Costello and her friends, there was a great deal said about poor little Miss Miller's going really 'too far.' Winterbourne was not pleased with what he heard, but when he saw Daisy get into an open cab* with her accomplice* and roll away through the streets of Rome, he could not deny to himself that she was going very far indeed.

- **accomplice:** partner in a crime or dishonest action
- **cab:** hired carriage
- **colonists:** people who live in a colony; expatriots
- **engaged:** promised in marriage, due to marry someone
- **marchese:** (Italian) marquis (noble person)
- **pilasters:** columns
- **taken him up:** accepted him

One day he met a friend in the Corso •, a tourist like himself. His friend talked for a moment about the superb portrait of Innocent X by Velasquez, which hangs in one of the cabinets • of the Doria Palace, and then said, 'And in the same cabinet, by the way, I had the pleasure of contemplating • a picture of a different kind – that pretty American girl whom you pointed out • to me last week.' His friend narrated that the pretty American girl – prettier than ever – was seated with a companion in the secluded nook • in which the great papal portrait was enshrined •.

'Who was her companion?' asked Winterbourne.

'A little Italian with a bouquet in his buttonhole.'

Having assured himself that his informant had seen Daisy and her companion only five minutes before, he jumped into a cab and went to call on Mrs Miller.

'Daisy's gone out somewhere with Mr Giovanelli,' said Mrs Miller. 'It seems as if they couldn't live without each other!' said Mrs Miller. 'Well, he's a real gentleman. I keep telling Daisy she's engaged!'

'And what does Daisy say?'

'Oh, she says she isn't engaged. But I've made Mr Giovanelli promise to tell me, if *she* doesn't. I should want to write to Mr Miller about it – shouldn't you?'

Winterbourne replied that he certainly should. But he felt that Daisy's mamma's way of thinking was so strange a way for a parent to think that he felt it would be hopeless to attempt to put her on her guard •.

Glossary

- **cabinets:** corners; small enclosed spaces or areas
- **contemplating:** looking at
- **Corso:** one of the main streets
- **enshrined:** kept safe; kept as if in a shrine
- **nook:** corner
- **put her on her guard:** warn her to be careful
- **pointed out:** showed; indicated

10 Daisy was never at home, and Winterbourne ceased to meet her at the houses of their common* acquaintances, because these shrewd* people had made up their minds that she was going too far. They ceased to invite her; and they said that they desired to tell observant Europeans that, though Miss Daisy Miller was a young American lady, her behaviour was not representative of American girls – was regarded by her compatriots as abnormal. Winterbourne wondered how she felt about all the cold shoulders* that were turned towards her. He asked himself whether Daisy's defiance* came from the consciousness of innocence, or from her being, essentially, a young person of the reckless class. He did not know how far her eccentricities were generic*, national, and how far they were personal. He had somehow missed her, and now it was too late. She was 'carried away' by Mr Giovanelli.

A few days after his brief interview with her mother, he encountered Daisy in the Palace of the Caesars. She was strolling along the top of one of the great ruins. It seemed to him also that Daisy had never looked so pretty, but this had been an observation of his whenever he met her. Giovanelli was at her side.

'Well,' said Daisy, 'You are always going round by yourself. Can't you get anyone to walk with you?'

'I am not so fortunate,' said Winterbourne, 'as your companion.'

Glossary

- **cold shoulders:** rejections; unfriendly behaviour expressed (towards someone)
- **common:** (here) who they both knew
- **defiance:** resistance
- **generic:** (here) shared by girls of her age and class
- **shrewd:** clever; crafty

Daisy Miller

Giovanelli, from the first, had treated Winterbourne with distinguished politeness. He carried himself in no degree like a jealous wooer•. On this occasion he strolled away from his companion to pick a piece of almond blossom, which he carefully arranged in his buttonhole.

'I know why you say that,' said Daisy, watching Giovanelli. 'Because you think I go round too much with *him*.'

'Every one thinks so – if you care to know,' said Winterbourne.

'Of course I care to know!' Daisy exclaimed seriously. 'But I don't believe it. They are only pretending to be shocked.'

'I think you will find they do care. They will show it unkindly.'

'How unkindly?'

'They will give you the cold shoulder. Do you know what that means?'

Daisy was looking at him intently; she began to colour. 'Do you mean as Mrs Walker did the other night?'

'Exactly!' said Winterbourne.

'I shouldn't think you would let people be so unkind!' she said.

'How can I help• it?' he asked.

'I should think you would say something.'

'I do say something'; and he paused a moment. 'I say that your mother tells me that she believes you are engaged.'

'Since you have mentioned it,' she said, 'I *am* engaged.'

Winterbourne looked at her. 'You don't believe it!' she added.

'Yes, I believe it,' he said.

'Oh, no, you don't!' she answered. 'Well, then – I am not!'

• **help:** (here) stop

• **wooer:** a man who is spending time with a lady giving her presents and making her promises in the hope that she will marry him

A week afterward Winterbourne went to dine at a beautiful villa on the Caelian Hill. The evening was charming, and he promised himself the satisfaction of walking home beneath the Arch of Constantine and past the vaguely lighted monuments of the Forum. When, on his return from the villa (it was eleven o'clock), Winterbourne approached the Colosseum, it recurred to him that the interior, in the pale moonshine, would be well worth a glance, even though its air was known to be unhealthy at night. He walked to one of the empty arches, near which an open carriage was stationed. Then he passed among the shadows

Daisy Miller

of the great structure, and emerged into the clear and silent arena. One half of the gigantic circus was in deep shade, the other was sleeping in the dusk. Winterbourne walked to the middle of the arena, to take a more general glance. The great cross in the centre was covered with shadow. Then he saw that two persons were positioned upon the low steps which formed its base. One of these was a woman, seated; her companion was standing in front of her.

Presently the sound of the woman's voice came to him distinctly in the warm night air in the familiar accent of Miss Daisy Miller.

Winterbourne stopped, with a sort of horror, and, it must be added, with a sort of relief. Miss Miller was a young lady whom a gentleman need no longer be at pains to• respect. He felt angry with himself that he had bothered so much about the right way of regarding Miss Daisy Miller. Then, as he was going to advance again, he checked himself. He turned away towards the entrance of the place, but, as he did so, he heard Daisy speak again.

REALISATION

Trois Couronnes, Rue d'Italie, Vevey

Think of a time when you suddenly understood or realised that what you had been doing was wrong.
What was the situation?
How did your attitude change?

Glossary

- **be at pains to:** take the trouble to

Daisy Miller

'Why, it was Mr Winterbourne! He saw me, and he cuts° me!'

Winterbourne came forward again and went towards the great cross. Daisy had got up; Giovanelli lifted his hat. Winterbourne had now begun to think simply of the craziness, from a sanitary° point of view, of a delicate young girl lounging away the evening in this nest of malaria. 'How long have you been here?' he asked almost brutally.

Daisy, lovely in the flattering° moonlight, looked at him a moment. 'All the evening,' she answered, gently. 'I never saw anything so pretty.'

'I am afraid,' said Winterbourne, 'that you will not think Roman fever very pretty. This is the way people catch it. I wonder,' he added, turning to Giovanelli, 'that you, a native Roman, should make such a mistake.'

'Ah,' said the handsome native, 'for myself I am not afraid.'

'Neither am I – for you! I am speaking for this young lady.'

'I told the signorina° it was a grave indiscretion°,' said Giovanelli, 'but when was the signorina ever prudent°?'

'I never was sick, and I don't mean to be!' the signorina declared. 'I don't look especially strong, but I'm healthy! I was bound to see the Colosseum by moonlight, and we have had the most beautiful time, haven't we, Mr Giovanelli? If there has been any danger, Eugenio can give me some pills°. He has got some splendid pills.'

- **cuts:** (here) ignores
- **flattering:** that makes her look nice
- **grave indiscretion:** silly thing to do
- **pills:** tablets; medicine in the form of small sweet-shaped things
- **prudent:** careful
- **sanitary:** health
- **signorina:** (Italian) young unmarried girl or woman

'I should advise you,' said Winterbourne, 'to drive home as fast as possible and take one!'

'What you say is very wise,' Giovanelli added. 'I will go and make sure the carriage is at hand°' And he went forward rapidly.

Daisy followed with Winterbourne. He kept looking at her; she seemed not in the least embarrassed. Daisy chattered about the beauty of the place. 'Well, I *have* seen the Colosseum by moonlight!' she exclaimed. 'That's one good thing.' Then, noticing Winterbourne's silence, she asked him why he didn't speak. He made no answer; he only began to laugh. They passed under one of the dark archways; Giovanelli was in front of the carriage. Here Daisy stopped a moment, looking at the young American. '*Did* you believe I was engaged, the other day?' she asked.

'I believe that it makes very little difference whether you are engaged or not!'

He felt the young girl's pretty eyes fixed upon him through the thick gloom° of the archway; she was apparently going to answer. But Giovanelli hurried her forward. 'Quick! quick!' he said; 'if we get in by midnight we are quite safe.'

Daisy took her seat in the carriage, and the fortunate Italian placed himself beside her. 'Don't forget Eugenio's pills!' said Winterbourne as he lifted his hat.

'I don't care,' said Daisy in a little strange tone, 'whether I have Roman fever or not!' Upon this the cab driver cracked his whip, and they rolled away.

Glossary

- **at hand:** nearby
- **thick gloom:** darkness

Daisy Miller

Winterbourne mentioned to no one that he had encountered Miss Miller, at midnight, in the Colosseum with a gentleman; but nevertheless, a couple of days later, the fact of her having been there under these circumstances was known to every member of the little American circle, and commented accordingly.

GOSSIP

Trois Couronnes, Rue d'Italie, Vevey

People in the story talk a lot about Daisy Miller but little to her.
Think of a time when you heard gossip about someone else. Were you interested? Did you tell the gossip to anyone else? What do you think of people who gossip?

They had of course known it at the hotel, and, after Daisy's return, there had been an exchange of remarks between the porter* and the cab driver. But the young man was conscious, at the same moment, that it had ceased to be a matter of serious regret* to him that the little American flirt should be 'talked about' by low-minded menials*.

Glossary

- **low-minded menials:** unintelligent or stupid people working in jobs that are not important
- **porter:** doorman at a hotel
- **regret:** (here) displeasure

Daisy Miller

These people, a day or two later, had serious information to give: the little American flirt was alarmingly • ill. Winterbourne, when the rumour came to him, immediately went to the hotel for more news. He found that two or three charitable • friends had preceded • him, and that they were being entertained in Mrs Miller's salon by Randolph.

'It's going round at night,' said Randolph – 'that's what made her sick. She's always going round at night.' Mrs Miller was invisible; she was now, at least, giving her daughter the advantage of her society. It was evident that Daisy was dangerously ill.

Winterbourne went often to ask for news of her, and once he saw Mrs Miller, who was perfectly calm. 'Daisy spoke of you the other day,' she said to him. 'Half the time she doesn't know what she's saying, but that time I think she did. She gave me a message she told me to tell you. She told me to tell you that she never was engaged to that handsome Italian. I am sure I am very glad; Mr Giovanelli hasn't been near us since she was taken ill. I thought he was so much of a gentleman; but I don't call that very polite! A lady told me that he was afraid I was angry with him for taking Daisy round at night. Well, so I am, but I suppose he knows I'm a lady, and of course I wouldn't think it correct to show my anger towards him. Anyway, she says she's not engaged.

I don't know why she wanted you to know, but she said to me three times, "Remember to tell Mr Winterbourne." And then she told me to ask if you remembered the time you went to that castle in Switzerland.'

• **alarmingly:** in a worrying way
• **charitable:** kind

• **preceded:** arrived before

But, as Winterbourne had said, it made very little difference. A week after this, the poor girl died; it had been a terrible case of the fever. Daisy's grave was in the little Protestant cemetery, beneath the cypresses and the thick spring flowers. Winterbourne stood there beside it, with a number of other mourners, a number larger than the scandal excited by the young lady's career would have led you to expect. Near him stood Giovanelli. He was very pale: on this occasion he had no flower in his buttonhole; he seemed to wish to say something. At last he said, 'She was the most beautiful young lady I ever saw, and the friendliest'; and then he added, 'and she was the most innocent.'

Winterbourne looked at him and repeated his words, 'And the most innocent?'

Daisy Miller

   Winterbourne felt sore and angry. 'Why,' he asked, 'did you take her to that fatal place?'
   Mr Giovanelli looked on the ground a moment, and then he said, 'For myself I had no fear; and she wanted to go.'
   'That was no reason!' Winterbourne declared.
   'If she had lived, I should have got nothing. She would never have married me, I am sure.'
   'She would never have married you?'
   'For a moment I had hoped so. But no. I am sure.'
   When Winterbourne turned away again, Mr Giovanelli, with his light, slow step, had departed.

Winterbourne almost immediately left Rome; but the following summer he again met his aunt, Mrs Costello at Vevey. In the interval Winterbourne had often thought of Daisy Miller and her mystifying manners•. One day he spoke of her to his aunt – said it was on his conscience• that he had done her injustice.

'I am sure I don't know,' said Mrs Costello. 'How did your injustice affect her?'

'She sent me a message before her death which I didn't understand at the time; but I have understood it since. She would have appreciated my esteem•.'

'Is that a modest way,' asked Mrs Costello, 'of saying that she would have reciprocated your affection• ?'

Winterbourne offered no answer to this question; but he said, 'You were right in that remark that you made last summer. I couldn't help making a mistake. I have lived too long in foreign parts.'

Nevertheless, he went back to live in Geneva, from where the most contradictory accounts• of his reasons for staying there continue to come: a report that he is 'studying' hard – an indication that he is much interested in a very clever foreign lady.

Glossary

- **accounts:** descriptions
- **esteem:** respect
- **it was on his conscience:** he felt guilty
- **manners:** way of behaving herself
- **reciprocated your affection:** felt affectionate to you as well

After Reading

Comprehension

1 **The language used by Henry James is elegant, but old-fashioned. Match the sentences in the first column of the table with the more modern equivalents in the second column.**

Henry James' language	Contemporary language
a) He was at liberty to wander about.	**1** He was about twenty-seven years old.
b) He was some seven-and-twenty years of age.	**2** I don't want to meet her.
c) She was much disposed toward conversation.	**3** Lunch is ready.
d) I have the honour to inform mademoiselle that luncheon is upon the table.	**4** She enjoyed talking to people.
e) I must decline the honour of her acquaintance.	**5** Why didn't you come to see me?
f) I suffer from the liver.	**6** He was free to go where he liked.
g) You might have come to see me!	**7** I have liver problems.

2 **Choose the correct answers.**

a) Winterbourne came to Vevey in order to
1) ☐ visit an ancient castle.
2) ☐ stay with his aunt.
3) ☐ take a break from studying in Geneva.

After Reading

b) When Winterbourne first meets Daisy, he notices that she
1) ☐ is not embarrassed.
2) ☐ does not look at him.
3) ☐ dislikes talking.

c) Daisy and Winterbourne are alone during their visit to the castle because
1) ☐ Daisy wanted to be alone with Winterbourne.
2) ☐ The custodian was not on duty that day.
3) ☐ Winterbourne paid the custodian to leave them alone.

d) When Daisy asks why Winterbourne didn't contact her as soon as he arrived in Rome, he tells her he
1) ☐ was sick.
2) ☐ had to visit his aunt first.
3) ☐ has just got off the train.

e) Mr Giovanelli speaks very good English. How did he learn?
1) ☐ He attended a language school.
2) ☐ He practised his English with many rich American ladies.
3) ☐ Daisy taught him English.

3 **What did they say? Put the following sentences into direct speech:**
Example: She told him that they were going to Rome for the winter.
'We are going to Rome for the winter,' she said.
   a) Daisy went on to say that she wished Winterbourne would travel with them.
   b) Winterbourne mentioned to Mrs Costello that he had spent the afternoon at Chillon with Miss Daisy Miller.
   c) Mrs Walker declared that if he (Winterbourne) refused her this favour she would never speak to him again.

After Reading

Characters

1 What's the name of:
  a) the Miller family's courier?
  b) Mrs Miller's son?
  c) Winterbourne's aunt?
  d) Daisy and Randolph's mother?
  e) Winterbourne's American friend?
  f) Daisy's Italian friend?

2 Read these sentences. In each case who is being described?
  a) 'A tall handsome man, with a superb moustache, wearing a velvet morning coat and a brilliant watch chain …'

  b) 'She was dressed in white muslin, with a hundred frills, and knots of pale-coloured ribbon.'

  c) 'He had a handsome face, an artfully poised hat, a monocle in one eye, and a nosegay in his buttonhole.'

  d) She 'was dressed with extreme elegance; she had enormous diamonds in her ears'

  e) She was 'a widow with a fortune; a person of much distinction'.

3 Through which character's eyes do we see the story (the central intelligence)?

After Reading

4 **Here are some adjectives used in the story to describe Daisy and Winterbourne.**
Which words are used to describe which person?
Write the words in the correct boxes.

> reckless guilty dreadful nice puzzled innocent stiff
> handsome horrid pretty ignorant perplexed charming
> mean common embarrassed afraid crazy uncultivated

Daisy	Winterbourne

5 **Do you like or dislike Winterbourne? Give three reasons for your answer. Share with a partner.**

6 **What would you ask Daisy? Think of questions and ask and answer with a partner.**

7 **According to Mrs Walker, 'everyone' is talking about Miss Miller. Write down some things that they may be saying about her.**

8 **Imagine you are an American living in Rome. Write a letter home describing your impression of Daisy and what she does. Begin your letter like this:**

Everyone here is talking about a young lady, an American called Miss Daisy Miller. She is behaving very badly indeed. Yesterday …

79

After Reading

Plot and theme

1 **Look at the list of words and expressions that you made before reading the story (Page 8, exercise 1). Were they accurate?**

2 **Put these events from the story in the correct order.**
   a) ☐ At her party, Mrs Walker disapproves of Daisy's behaviour and turns her back on her.
   b) ☐ Daisy dies from the fever and is buried in Rome.
   c) ☐ Frederick Winterbourne meets Daisy Miller at a Swiss hotel while visiting his aunt, Mrs Costello.
   d) ☐ Daisy tells Winterbourne that she is engaged to Mr Giovanelli.
   e) ☐ Daisy falls ill, but delivers a message to Winterbourne that she was never engaged to Giovanelli.
   f) ☐ Winterbourne and Daisy visit the Castle of Chillon alone.
   g) ☐ Winterbourne meets Daisy and Giovanelli at night at the Colosseum.

3 **In the story, what kind of attitude does the American community in Rome have towards Italians? Find comments in the text to support your answer.**

4 **Write a new ending to the story. Begin from this episode.**
   It was dark, but Winterbourne saw that two people were sitting on the steps. He recognised the woman's voice. It was Daisy Miller ...

5 **Daisy is described as being 'innocent'. Find examples of her innocence in the text. Share with a partner.**

6 **In *Daisy Miller* Henry James explores man's inhumanity to man. Find examples of this in the story.**